ME TOO!

Holiday House • New York

Two Small Stories About Small Animals

Retold and illustrated by Katya Arnold Based on stories by V. Suteev

3

Me Too!

Duckling
pushed his
way out
of the egg.
"I hatched," he said.

"Me, too,"
said Chick.

"I'm going
for a walk,"
said Duckling.

"Me,
too,"
said Chick.

"I like digging a hole,"
said Duckling.

"Me, too,"

said Chick.

"I found a tasty worm," said Duckling.

"I'm going
for a swim,"
said Duckling.

"Me,
too,"
said Chick.

"I'm swimming,"
said Duckling.

"Me, too!"
shouted Chick.
And she jumped in....

Duckling dived down and pulled Chick out of the water.

"Another swim?"
asked Duckling.

"*Not me!*"

said Chick.

Three Kittens

Three kittens—
gray, black,
and white— *saw a mouse and chased after her.*

The kittens jumped after her...

She ran
away...

...and three **white**
kittens climbed
out of the canister.

Three white kittens chased a frog into a dirty old pipe...

The
frog
hopped
away...

...and three **black** kittens climbed out of the pipe.

The fish
swam away...

...and three **wet**
kittens got out
of the water.

They dried and were

gray, black, and white

as they always were.

To Alexander and his brave parents,
Simone and Owen, with love.
K. A.

Acknowledgments

Thanks to Regina Griffin, for her encouragement and tireless praise of my pictures. Thanks to Simone Kaplan, who, as a fan of Vladimir Suteev's stories, helped me with the selection and the English retellings. And finally, many thanks to Yvette Lenhart, for her sensitivity and patience during our collaboration on all of Suteev's projects.

Author's Note

Vladimir Suteev was a hugely successful artist, writer, movie director, and producer. He was born in 1903 and became a kind of Russian Walt Disney. His films are sweet, funny, and full of action-packed adventure. Suteev was also famous for his many picture books, some originals and others based on his films. This dual talent might be explained by the fact that Suteev wrote with his left hand and drew with his right!

Me Too! is based on two of Suteev's stories, "Chick and Duckling," and "Three Kittens," which are beloved by Russian children. I hope that these humorous and joyful stories will become favorites of American parents and children alike.

Colophon

The original black line drawings for this book were reproduced on acetate. Then the artist painted the color on the underside of the acetate using acrylic paint. The backgrounds were prepared with watercolors. To achieve the final effect, the artist positioned the acetate paintings over the watercolors.

Copyright © 2000 by Katya Arnold
All Rights Reserved
Printed in the United States of America
First Edition

Library of Congress Cataloging-in-Publication Data

Arnold, Katya

Me too!: two small stories about small animals/
retold and illustrated by Katya Arnold; based on stories
by V. Suteev—1st edition
p.   cm.

Contents: Me too!—Three Kittens.
Summary: In two separate stories, different animals
learn that copying others is not always a good idea.

ISBN 0-8234-1483-3

1. Children's stories, American.
[1. Animals—Fiction. 2. Ducks—Fiction. 3. Chickens—Fiction.
4. Cats—Fiction. 5. Short stories.]
I. Suteev, V. (Vladimir) II. Title: Me Too!.
III. Title: Three kittens. IV. Title.

PZ7.A7356Mc   2000

[E]—dc21   99-016696

Design: Yvette Lenhart